Book Club Edition

WALT DISNEY PRODUCTIONS

presents

Three Aristocats in Trouble

Random House  New York

Duchess the Aristocat and O'Malley
the alley cat were going out for the day.
"We'll be back at five o'clock sharp,"
said O'Malley.
O'Malley lived with Duchess and her
three kittens, Tu-Tu, Marie, and Berly.
They all lived in Madame's big house.

"Now remember, Tu-Tu," said Duchess,
"practice your painting! Marie, practice
your singing! Berly, practice your piano!"
"We will," they all answered.

The three Aristocats watched Duchess
and O'Malley walk away.

They kept their noses pressed
against the window.
 Finally Duchess and O'Malley
were out of sight.

"I know the kittens will be good,"
declared Duchess.
"I hope you are right!" said O'Malley.

Back at the house, the three kittens marched up the stairs.

Marie started singing.

Berly played the piano.

And Tu-Tu painted.

But soon Tu-Tu got bored.
He crept over to the piano . . .

and squirted paint on Berly!
Tu-Tu thought that was funny.
And so did Berly.
What a mess they made!

Marie heard the fuss.
"Listen to me sing!" she called out.
"La la la . . ."

"Listen to us play!" said Tu-Tu.
What a noise they made!

Then Tu-Tu said,
"Let's take a ride!"
So they slid down
the banister . . .

right into Madame's best vase...
and right up to the door!

"Now let's go for a walk," said
Tu-Tu the troublemaker.

"We really shouldn't," said Berly.
"We are not allowed."
"But let's go anyway," said Marie.
So they did.

Outside, the kittens looked at the
busy street.
They saw people, trucks, and cars.
Crossing this street would be scary!

They dashed out into the road . . .
and reached the other side, just in time.

"That was close!" said Marie.
"Maybe we should go home," said Berly.
"Of course not, 'fraidy cat," said Tu-Tu.
So on they went.

But suddenly the three kittens saw a
big dog coming toward them.

"I'll take care of him!" whispered Tu-Tu.

"Hissss!" spat Tu-Tu.

"Rowf!" barked the dog.

"What a nasty dog!" cried Tu-Tu.

"Quick! This way!"
said Berly.
The three kittens quickly
climbed a nearby fence.

"Close again!" said Berly, panting.
"We have had enough close calls,"
said Marie. "It is time to go home."
"Are you a 'fraidy cat too?" asked
Tu-Tu. "I am not ready to go home yet."

So the three kittens walked
over to the river.

Suddenly a big striped cat came up
to them.

"Hi there," he said. "If you are out
for adventure, come with me."

The three kittens huddled together.

"Mother says never to talk to strangers," whispered Marie.

"But we're looking for adventure!" said Tu-Tu.

So off they went.

The big cat took them to his alley.
"Meet my friends," said the big cat.

These cats looked mean!

"Let's go home!" cried Berly.
This time Tu-Tu did not call
him a 'fraidy cat.
He ran away as fast as
Marie and Berly did.
The alley cats laughed loudly.

The kittens ran on and on.
They ran past a policeman.

They ran past
a fountain.

At last they
were home!
In they went,
all at once!

"We are very messy!" cried Berly.
The naughty kittens knew they
would be in trouble.

"We must clean up before Mother
and O'Malley come home," said
Marie.

Marie cleaned her paws on
the couch.
    Berly cleaned his paws on
the drapes.

Tu-Tu rolled
around on the
footstool.

When Duchess and O'Malley came
home, there sat the kittens, clean as
could be.

They were quietly reading.

"Hello, dears," said Duchess.

"I hope you were
good little kittens
while we were gone."

Just then Madame walked in.
She was very angry.
She had seen the dirty couch,
the dirty drapes, and the dirty
footstool.

She had seen the broken vase and
the red piano keys.
She blamed O'Malley the alley cat.
"You miserable cat!" she said to
poor O'Malley.

But the kittens knew Madame was wrong.
"Oh no!" they cried. "We are the ones
who made the mess! Then we ran away
and played."
But Madame did not understand them.
She walked away in a huff.

"You made the mess?" cried Duchess.
"You ran away? Then you are very
naughty kittens."

"But wait," said O'Malley. "They may
be naughty sometimes, but they always
tell the truth."

"So they do," Duchess agreed. "I
will forgive them. But they must never
do this again."

And then the three tired kittens
happily had their supper.